G Artichoke Murder

Book Eleven

in

Papa Pacelli's Pizzeria Series

By

Patti Benning

Copyright 2017 Summer Prescott Books

Author's Note: On the next page, you'll find out how to access all of my books easily, as well as locate books by best-selling author, Summer Prescott. I'd love to hear your thoughts on my books, the storylines, and anything else that you'd like to comment on – reader feedback is very important to me. Please see the following page for my publisher's contact information. If you'd like to be on her list of "folks to contact" with updates, release and sales notifications, etc...just shoot her an email and let her know. Thanks for reading!

Also...

...if you're looking for more great reads, from me and Summer, check out the Summer Prescott Publishing Book Catalog:

http://summerprescottbooks.com/book-catalog/ for some truly delicious stories.

Contact Info for Summer Prescott Publishing:

Twitter: @summerprescott1

Blog and Book Catalog: http://summerprescottbooks.com

Email: summer.prescott.cozies@gmail.com

And...look up The Summer Prescott Fan Page and Summer Prescott Publishing Page on Facebook – let's be friends!

To sign up for our fun and exciting newsletter, which will give you opportunities to win prizes and swag, enter contests, and be the first to know about New Releases, click here:

https://forms.aweber.com/form/02/1682036602.htm

TABLE OF CONTENTS

Garlic Artichoke

MURDER

Book Eleven in Papa Pacelli's Pizzeria Series

CHAPTER ONE

T he ocean was dotted with sailboats, and the water sparkled. Traffic on the road that wound along the Maine coast was heavy with the first tourists of the season, and the scents of burning coals and roasting hot dogs permeated the air as families celebrated the first truly hot week of the year.

Eleanora Pacelli noticed none of that. Her thoughts were on something that she had found in her boyfriend's pocket the week before. She could think of only one reason for Russell Ward to have a ring box in his pocket, and she wasn't sure how she felt about the implications.

She wasn't sure whether the fact that he hadn't mentioned it yet was good or bad. She had deliberately avoided him since her discovery, and feared that he would notice her odd behavior if they spent time together. She knew she couldn't avoid him forever, but right now she couldn't even look at him without feeling panic well up in her chest.

A ring. Marriage. Was she ready for any of that? Was she ready for that with him? Was *he* really ready for it? He was a widower who had lived alone since his wife was murdered years ago. The only creature he shared his home with was a cat, and Sookie was a recent, accidental acquisition.

That brought up another problem. Where would they live? Right now, Ellie shared a house with her eighty-five-year-old grandmother. Ann Pacelli was healthy for a woman of her age, but even so, Ellie wouldn't be comfortable with Nonna living on her own. Yet the thought of Russell moving into the Pacelli house was absurd. She could, she supposed, stop in to visit the older woman every day, supposing they got a place in town.

Stop it, she told herself. *I don't even know if he's going to propose. I could be wrong about what I thought I felt in the pocket. I hope I was wrong. Or do I?* She was confused by her own feelings on the matter. She had only known the man for a year. True, they complemented each other beautifully, but she had already come to

11

realize that she wasn't necessarily the best judge of men. Her last relationship had ended in tears when she discovered her fiancé with another woman. She couldn't imagine Russell betraying her trust like that, but then she hadn't thought her ex would cheat on her either.

She desperately needed to talk to someone about everything. The only problem was, her best friend also happened to be Russell's sister-in-law. If she was wrong about the whole thing and Shannon let something slip, well, Ellie didn't know if she would ever be able to face the Ward family again.

Talking to Nonna was another option, but the elderly woman was probably more likely than Shannon to mention something to her friends. She wouldn't mean it badly, of course, but gossip was like water to the women who met every week for lunch at the nursing home—where half of them lived.

Ellie had kept her discovery a secret for the better part of a week, but the urge to confide in someone had finally grown too strong to resist. That was why she was on her way over to Shannon's house. She would just have to ask her friend not to tell anyone, even her husband. She would lose her mind if she didn't find reassurance somewhere.

Shannon and James Ward lived in a beautiful house in one of the newer suburbs in the small town of Kittiport. James was a contractor, and was exceptionally busy this time of year. Shannon, who worked at the local newspaper, had a more flexible schedule. She had been more than happy to invite Ellie over for lunch, and Ellie had been happy to supply the food.

She knocked at the front door half an hour after leaving her home, with a warm pizza box in one hand and a two-liter bottle of cold soda in the other. Owning a pizzeria had its perks, and Papa Pacelli's wasn't just any pizzeria; it served the best pizza in the area.

"Come on in," Shannon shouted through the door. Ellie turned the knob and stepped into a brutally air-conditioned living room. She shut the door behind her and followed the sound of clacking to the kitchen, where she found her friend typing on a laptop.

"I brought lunch," she said, setting the pizza down on the table. "Garlic artichoke pizza with white sauce. I know you like garlic."

"That sounds delicious. I'm almost done with this article. Can you grab plates and stuff while I finish up the last paragraph?"

Ellie knew the layout of her friend's kitchen well enough to find the plates and glasses on the first try. By the time she had set two places on the table, the other woman had shut her laptop and was opening the pizza box.

"So, what's tomorrow's news?" Ellie asked. "Anything interesting?"

"I was just doing a column on the weekend's activities. The farmers market will be opening, a local band is playing in the park, and on Sunday there's a wedding at the community center, so the food drive is being moved to the library."

"Ah, small town life," the pizzeria owner said. "I'm sure Nonna will want to go to the farmer's market. Last year she fell in love with the pies one of the vendors makes."

"James and I will be there too," Shannon said. "I'm taking pictures for the paper, and I'm dragging him along. You should see if Russ is free too, and we can grab lunch after and make a day out of it."

"Or pack something to eat and take the *Eleanora* out if it's a nice day," Ellie suggested. The *Eleanora* was her grandfather's boat. He had named it after her, and had left it to her grandmother when he passed.

"That would be wonderful. Do you think Russ will be able to make it? I can tell James to make sure his schedule is clear all afternoon."

"I don't know. I don't think he has any major cases at the moment, but I haven't seen much of him the past few days."

"I guess he's probably been busy dealing with all of the craziness that went down at the pizzeria last week. Speaking of that, did your window get replaced yet?"

"Yes. James came through, like always. You married a great man."

Shannon smiled. "I know."

Ellie was suddenly reminded of her reason for coming over. She focused on serving herself a piece of pizza as she tried to figure out how to bring up what was on her mind.

"This might sound crazy," she began, "but Russell lent me his jacket a few days ago, and… I thought I felt something in the pocket."

Her friend raised her eyebrows. "Like what? A gun? You know he carries."

Russell was the town's sheriff, and almost always had a firearm within reach. Ellie understood why; she had seen enough of the town's frightening underside that she didn't question it. He had already been shot once in the time that she had known him, and had been shot at again the week before, although thankfully that bullet had missed him.

"No, something else." She bit her lip, regretting bringing it up at all, but knowing that it was too late to back out now. "I thought I felt a ring box."

A look of mild surprise flashed across her friend's face. It was enough to tell Ellie that if Russell was planning on proposing, he hadn't mentioned it to his sister-in-law.

"I was probably imagining things," she said. "Just don't tell anyone I mentioned it, okay? I would be so embarrassed."

"I don't know," Shannon mused. "I mean, of course I won't tell anyone, but I don't know if you were imagining it. I know Russ is crazy for you."

"I just haven't been able to look at him without thinking about it," Ellie said. "I feel bad for avoiding him, but he's going to notice if I act a little bonkers around him. We went out for coffee while I was waiting for Nonna to get out of physical therapy a couple of days ago, and the entire time I was there, I was terrified that he was going to pop the question."

"Terrified? Do you want him to propose?" Shannon asked. "What would you say?"

"I don't know," Ellie admitted. "I keep going back and forth, and I don't even know if he's going to ask. I'm probably freaking myself out over nothing. I just needed to tell someone."

"Don't stress over it so much. I honestly don't know what his plans are, but I doubt he'd ask unless he's almost certain you will say yes. He's a careful guy, and he doesn't want to risk messing up your relationship. I think you should just try to relax around him and spend more time together."

17

"I'll try," Ellie said. "If we can all go out on the boat on Saturday, that would be nice. You're right that I need to relax. It looks like it's going to be a beautiful summer; the pizzeria is doing better than ever now that Cheesaroni Calzones closed down; and I've really got nothing to worry about other than the man I love possibly proposing to me."

She laughed, but as she took a sip of her soda, she couldn't help but feel that same persistent twinge of anxiety. She didn't know if she was ready to get married, and if Russell asked and she said no, could their relationship possibly survive?

CHAPTER TWO

The wonderful late spring weather finally inspired Ellie that evening. Instead of making dinner inside, she found her grandfather's ancient grill in the garage, dragged it outside, cleaned it, and filled it with equally ancient charcoal. It took her a couple of tries to get it lit, but soon enough the coals were turning white and the grill was ready for the corn on the cob, bratwurst, and chopped-up veggies she had bought on the way home from Shannon's house.

She and Nonna spent the evening sitting in lawn chairs in the back yard, eating barbecue to their heart's content while Bunny—Ellie's little black and white papillon—rolled in the freshly cut grass.

Ellie sat up long enough to lower the back of her lawn chair, then leaned back and closed her eyes, overcome with a sense of peace.

She really was happy here. Maybe that was why she was so worried about what might have been a ring in Russell's pocket; getting engaged would mean change, and she really didn't want anything to change just then. Her life was as close to perfect as it ever had been. How could anything, even marriage, make it better?

Her sense of peace lasted until—as she drove toward the pizzeria after filling up on gasoline in town—she saw that the *For Sale* sign in the window of the calzone shop had been exchanged for a *Sold* sign.

The men that had owned and run the calzone shop had spent months tormenting her and trying their hardest to bring Papa Pacelli's to its knees. She had been relieved when the shop had finally shut its doors. Now, it looked like another restaurant would be taking its place.

What are the chances that the people who bought it will be as petty and cruel as Jeffrey and Xavier? she reassured herself. *The new owners will likely be perfectly nice people.*

Still, she couldn't help but think that the sign was something of an ominous omen that change was coming whether she wanted it or not.

Papa Pacelli's was only a block away from the marina, and in the fall and winter, when the trees were naked, she could see the harbor just by sticking her head out the door. With the trees fully leafy, the water was now hidden from view, but the fresh sea breeze still reached the outdoor patio she had installed earlier in the year.

Today the streets were busy with both cars and pedestrians, and she had barely turned the sign on when her first customers came in. They seated themselves outside, and she brought them ice-cold glasses of fresh lemonade while they looked over the menu. Iris, whose brightly colored hair was a shocking mixture of pink and green this week, took their orders while Ellie seated the next group. It was going to be a busy day, but she didn't mind. There was nowhere she would rather be.

By the time Jacob came in at five, they were sorely in need of his help. Ellie was grateful for the chance to get off her feet and work the register. She was thrilled and amazed at how well the pizzeria was doing. Not for the first time, she entertained the idea of opening a second store, but the same problems that she ran into every time she thought about it were still there.

If she wanted to ensure that the new store wouldn't steal business and customers from the original Papa Pacelli's, she'd have to open it at least an hour away from Kittiport, if not further. While her employees were wonderful and knew their way around the pizza shop, she didn't know if any of them were ready for the task of managing a store, but she couldn't very well run two stores at once, at least not for long. If it was just her, she might be able to move to the new store's location while it got up and running, but she couldn't leave Nonna alone.

If she had someone she could trust to run one of the stores smoothly while she focused on the other, things might be different. In a year or two, Jacob might be up for that job; she would just have to wait until then.

The bell on the door jingled and she pulled her thoughts away from the future to greet the customer—then saw that it was Russell. *What is he doing here?* she wondered. It wasn't unusual for him to stop in if he was passing by, but lately she had been so on edge around him that she found herself questioning even the little things. *I really wish I had never put that jacket on*, she thought. *I don't know how I'll ever relax around him if I think he's going to pull out a ring any second.*

"Hey," she said, smiling at him despite her worries. It *was* good to see him.

"Hey. I figured you'd be in here today. I saw how full the parking lot is. I'm glad to see this place is doing well."

"I wish my grandfather was around to see it. He would be impressed. Oh, before I forget, Shannon and I are trying to plan an outing on Saturday afternoon. We thought we'd all go to the farmer's market together, then pack up some food and have lunch on the *Eleanora* if it's nice out. Can you make it?"

It would be the perfect way to spend some time together without her worrying about a proposal. Russell was a private person, and she doubted he would propose when they were around others, even if those others were his family.

"I should be able to. I actually stopped in to see what your plans are for this weekend too. A friend of mine is getting married on Sunday.

He sent me the invitation a while ago, and it slipped my mind until I got an email reminder. Would you be able to go with me? I know it's short notice, but the wedding is just at the community center and it shouldn't be an all-day event."

A wedding? She bit her lip. It would be the perfect setting for a proposal. She rarely worked on the weekends, so unless something came up with Nonna, she wouldn't have any handy excuses. Besides, she would feel bad to make him go by himself.

"I'm completely free that day," she said. "I'd be happy to go with. What time does it start?"

"Two. The reception is after, and it'll be pretty laid back."

"I'll look forward to it," she said. "And I'll tell Shannon that Saturday is a go. It's shaping up to be a busy weekend."

"Busy," he said, "but fun. It will be nice to see more of each other, for a change. Our schedules just haven't seemed to align lately."

She felt a stab of guilt. Looking back on the week, she realized just how many times he had tried to invite her somewhere just for her to refuse. She really *was* looking forward to the weekend, ring or no ring. Russell was one of the best parts of her life, and she promised herself that she would stop trying to push him away.

PATTI BENNING

CHAPTER THREE

Ellie woke up early on Saturday morning; something that she normally avoided doing if she could. The evening before, Russell had called to ask if it was all right with her if his friend John, the man who was getting married the next day, and John's fiancée Rayleigh accompanied them on the *Eleanora*. Of course, she had said yes, but it had turned what would have otherwise been a relaxing outing with people she considered practically family into a more formal event.

Wanting to make a good impression on the soon-to-be newlyweds, Ellie decided to go all out with food preparation that day. Normally she would have just picked up a pizza at Papa Pacelli's before heading to the marina. Instead, she decided to make a variety of finger sandwiches at home beforehand, and also pack some of her grandmother's famous chocolate chip cookies.

28

Before moving home to Kittiport, Ellie had never spent much time cooking. She had been kept so busy by her accounting job that she usually just had time for microwavable meals and an occasional splurge on takeout or delivery. She had been surprised to discover that she actually enjoyed working in the kitchen. She was still amazed at the way a handful of raw ingredients could come together to form a tasty dish. From barely edible to mouthwatering was nothing short of magic. Once she had learned the basics, she had begun to experiment with adding her own twist to different recipes, and more often than not, the results were quite good.

She spent the morning preparing crust-less cucumber sandwiches, spreading homemade chicken salad, and arranging thin slices of deli meat and cheese on whole wheat bread. The cookies, which she and her grandmother had made the evening before, she packed into plastic containers, separating the layers with wax paper. Shannon would be bringing drinks, and the men had promised to supply the paper plates, napkins, and cups. Ellie knew that once she got on the boat, she would be able to relax, but for now all she could do was worry that one of them might forget something important. When they were a quarter of a mile away from the coast, it wouldn't exactly be a simple matter to pop back in and grab whatever it was they had forgotten from a store.

She had become something of a stickler for presentation; working at the pizzeria had taught her that the way food looked was almost as important as how it tasted. So, by the time the food was prepared to her satisfaction, the sun was well up into the beautiful, cloudless blue sky, promising another hot, clear day. She had gone out on the *Eleanora* enough to know that it could get chilly out on the water even if it was sweltering on land; the wind tended to really pick up out on the ocean, and the occasional salty spray of water also cooled things down.

She put on a pair of capris and a loose, short-sleeved top, then grabbed a light windbreaker from her closet. Bunny, who had been following her ever since she packed the food up, gave an excited yip when she saw Ellie add her tiny bright orange life vest to the pile of things going into the car.

"You didn't think I'd leave you behind, did you?" the pizzeria owner said. "You're coming along, as long as you promise to be good. Just because you're wearing a life vest doesn't mean it's safe for you to go overboard. Think of the sharks, Bunny. I hate to break it to you, but you're a bite-sized dog."

The papillon spun in an excited circle, unfazed by her owner's mention of sharks. Ellie grinned at the little dog's enthusiasm. She had no idea how such a small body managed to hold so much boundless energy, but Bunny was one companion who was always ready to go.

She met Shannon and James at the marina. The other woman had gone to the farmers market earlier in the day, to get photos while the stands and vendors were still fresh. Ellie felt a surge of admiration for her friend. Since they were children, Shannon had always wanted to be a journalist. She was living her dream, even if the paper she worked for served only a couple of the tiny towns that dotted their section of the coast.

"Did you get everything you needed for the article?" Ellie asked her friend as the two of them waited for Russell and their other two guests to arrive.

"I did. I think this is going to be a great year for the local hobby farms. It was busy, even though this early in the season there isn't much produce to choose from. Buying local goods seems to be getting more and more popular every year. I think part of that has to do with how affordable advertising has become. Vendors can create pages for free on social media and interact directly with their customers. It creates a feeling of community, which the big supermarkets are lacking."

"It sounds like you've been giving this some thought," Ellie said.

"I know a lot of my articles are about small, local things that aren't really important, but I still like to do research for them. One day I would love to work for a major paper, but I know that's probably a reach."

"Not at all. I think you're a great writer, and it's obvious that you care about what you do. I'm sure James would support you, even if you had to move for the job."

"Oh, I wouldn't want to leave Kittiport. This is my home."

Ellie smiled. She understood what her friend meant. The small town had a way of clinging to its residents. Even though she had spent most of her life out of the state, now that she was back she could hardly imagine relocating again. She would miss everything about the little town nestled on the Maine coast. For someone who had lived there her entire life, someone like Shannon, the thought of leaving must seem nearly impossible.

An old pickup truck pulled into the parking spot next to Ellie's car. She grinned and waved at the sheriff, who handed her a paper grocery bag filled with paper plates and plastic utensils before shutting off the engine and getting out.

"Where's your friend?" she asked. "I thought he would be meeting us here."

"I told John and Rayleigh to meet us at the boat. He helped your grandfather repaint it when Art first bought the thing; he'll be able to find it. They'll be here in about half an hour, but we can go ahead and get set up while we wait."

Ellie was surprised to hear that John had known her grandfather. She often forgot that Arthur Pacelli had been well-known around town. He had managed the paper mill that had employed a good percentage of the locals until it closed two decades ago. Even after the mill shut down, he had stayed in the public eye by opening the pizzeria. The knowledge that John had known her grandfather suddenly made her weirdly uncomfortable. For some reason, she always got a little nervous about meeting people who'd known her grandfather, as if she had to live up to his good example. It was silly, but she couldn't shake the feeling.

CHAPTER FOUR

The four of them made their way to the *Eleanora*, Bunny bopping along beside them. Russell helped Shannon onto the boat, then turned to take the cooler from Ellie. He handed the cooler to Shannon, then stepped onto the boat before offering Ellie his hand. James came last, tossing a couple of folding camp chairs onto the deck before jumping the gap himself.

The *Eleanora* was a beautiful white boat with a cabin and an expansive deck. Right now, it was bobbing gently in the waves like a patient dog. Ellie wasn't comfortable taking the boat out herself, but she enjoyed sunning herself on the deck while it was tied securely to the dock. One day she thought she might ask Russell or James teach her how to sail it, but for now she was happy going out with her friends.

Before Bunny had a chance to bounce overboard, Ellie strapped the life jacket to the dog, then unhooked her leash. Bunny went into the cabin and hopped up on one of the padded benches. She had been on the boat many times before, and knew all of the most comfortable places. Even falling into the ocean hadn't dampened her enthusiasm for adventure. Seeing her owner watching her, the little dog sat up and gave a yip of excitement. She was ready for whatever was to come.

Ellie had just begun taking the picnic supplies out of the cooler when two people approached the boat: a man with chestnut brown hair and matching eyes, with a broad smile on his face, and a woman in dark sunglasses a few inches shorter than Ellie. She pulled her auburn hair back into a ponytail as they approached, then flashed them a bright grin. The man took her hand, entwining his fingers with hers. They looked like the perfect, happy couple, and Ellie guessed that they were the soon-to-be newlyweds.

Russell went up to the man and shook his hand, then helped the woman onto the boat. Turning to Ellie, he said, "This is John and Rayleigh, his fiancée."

"Nice to meet you," Rayleigh said. "You can just call me Leigh. Everyone does."

"Thanks for inviting us out today," said John. "It'll be nice to take a breather before the wedding. I never expected how busy it would be, trying to plan everything."

"You should have kept it small. From what I've been hearing, half the town is planning on showing up," Shannon said, walking forward to give him a quick hug.

"It's too late to uninvite people," he said with a laugh. "We're both happy with a nice, big wedding. I'm just glad the planning stages are finally over. All that's left to do is get dressed in the morning, walk down the aisle, and then have a good time at the reception. How are you doing, by the way? It's been a while since I've seen you and James."

"I'm doing pretty well," she said. "I'm just glad to hear that you're finally getting married. It'll be great to see the two of you walk down the aisle together tomorrow."

The newcomers helped them finish setting up the food while Russell started the boat and eased them out of the marina, James acting as spotter. The large harbor was dotted with other boats; it seemed that they weren't the only ones with the idea to enjoy the day out on the water. They didn't start eating until they reached the open ocean, with a beautiful view of the Maine coast off the starboard side.

It was a perfect day. The sun was out, the skies were clear, and the waves lapped gently against the side of the boat in the gentle wind. Ellie smiled to see her friends enjoying the food that she had spent the morning making. Occasionally Bunny managed to beg tidbits from people, doing tricks for the attention as much as the food.

After they were finished eating, the men went out on the deck and set up the chairs before cracking open the cooler of drinks that Russell had brought. Ellie, Shannon, and Leigh stayed in the cabin to talk. Leigh seemed interested in the pizzeria, and Ellie learned that she used to enjoy eating there back when she lived in town.

"When did you move?" she asked as the three of them sipped their glasses of ice-cold raspberry lemonade.

"I moved away about six or seven years ago," she said. "I knew John for a while before I left, and we started talking over the internet and phone a few years ago after he went through a breakup. Eventually we met up and, well, things just went from there. I'll be moving back after we get married; I left for a job down in Portland—I'm a pharmacist—but I'm not super happy there. I'm glad I'll be able to have my wedding here. I always loved this town."

"Did you grow up here?" Ellie asked.

"I grew up in the area, but I was homeschooled," she explained. "I met Shannon through her church group back when we were teens. That's how I met John, in fact, through her. He was friends with the Ward brothers even back then, and often hung around with her, James, and a couple of other people our age. I always liked him, but it wasn't until we reconnected a couple of years ago that we realized the feelings were mutual."

"That's such a sweet story," Ellie said.

"It's the sort of thing that can only happen in a small town," Leigh said. "I actually used to date his best man, Damien. It's kind of funny to think back to how we were all those years ago. Who would have guessed how we would end up? At least we're all happy now. I'm glad that Russell has started dating again at last. It will be so nice to see the two of you at the wedding."

"I'm looking forward to it," Ellie said. "Do you have any big plans tonight?"

Leigh laughed. "No, not really. I know I should be having a bachelorette party, but I just don't feel like it. The last couple of weeks have been so busy, I just want one last relaxing evening before the big day."

"Are you nervous about the wedding?" Shannon asked.

Leigh paused to think about that for a second. "Not really, I guess," she answered. "Maybe I should be. I'm more worried about what comes after—moving, finding a new job I'm happy with, starting a whole new chapter of my life. It's a big leap to make, moving back across the state."

After a while, Ellie wandered out onto the deck and joined the men. They were talking about fishing, though none of them had brought poles with them today. Russell smiled when he saw her and stood

41

up to offer her his chair. She took it, and he stood behind her, his hand on her shoulder. She felt... happy. She realized she actually *was* looking forward to the wedding. It would be wonderful to see these two great people married. She wondered for a second if they might not be attending her own wedding in a year's time, then shook her head, telling herself to stop it. She was still unsure about the idea of getting married, and didn't even know if Russell was going to propose, for heaven's sake. She was getting ahead of herself. For now, it was enough to be happy for his friends. She didn't know if it was even possible for her life to get any better than it was right now, and she wasn't in any hurry to change anything.

CHAPTER FIVE

Ellie twisted around, trying to see the back of her dress in the bathroom mirror. It was an old dress, one that she hadn't worn in a while. Frankly, she was surprised it still fit. It was a beautiful light blue; the color reminded her of clear skies. The dress looked nice, but she wasn't sure about the rest of herself.

Her hair was difficult, as always. Straight, dark, and tough to style in anything other than a ponytail. She debated on leaving it down, but knew that she would regret it if it was humid out. She was envious of Leigh's beautiful hair, which looked like it would be easy to style however she wanted. She had exchanged phone numbers with the woman the day before, and planned on asking her who her hairstylist was when Leigh's life got a little less crazy.

It had been a while since she had gone to a wedding, so she wasn't quite sure what to expect from this one. She had only ever attended the weddings of close friends, and those had all been small events, but from what John had said, he and Leigh had invited quite a few people. She knew that she was bound to run into some familiar faces; it would almost be impossible to go to an event in town without seeing someone she recognized. She just hoped that her dress held up, that her hair stayed where it was supposed to, and that she didn't spill anything on herself.

Russell pulled into the driveway at one o'clock, wearing the nicest suit he owned. He cleaned up well. It wasn't her first time seeing him in fancy dress, but she was always surprised. Normally, when he wasn't in his sheriff's uniform, he was wearing something casual and comfortable. Today he had even shaved, and it was a pleasant shock to see his face so smooth.

He brushed a kiss across her lips when he saw her, telling her how beautiful she looked. She smiled at the compliment. She knew that she was average looking, but it was nice of him to say otherwise.

"If I had known about the wedding sooner, I would have bought something new," she told him. "I'm sure what I'm wearing is completely outdated."

"I've had this suit for eight years," he said with a chuckle. "Your dress is fine. And you look amazing."

"Maybe, if you squint and look at me sideways," she said, laughing. "At least all eyes will be on Leigh, not on me."

"Not *all* eyes," he said, and touched her nose. Before she could respond, he closed the passenger door and started around the front to the driver's side.

They managed to find a parking spot at the community center, even though the lot was filling up fast. Ellie realized with a jolt that the last time she had been inside the community center had been not long after a woman that she had known had been killed. Then, the building had been full of people taking refuge from a nasty winter storm. Now, it was almost unrecognizable.

It looked like John and Leigh had rented out the entire building. Every inch of the interior was decorated with white and gold. Soft white lights were draped across the rafters and wrapped around the columns at the entrance. Signs directed them to the room in which the wedding would take place and another set of signs pointed toward the basement room, where the reception would happen later. Russell paused to say hello to someone he knew, and Ellie waved to one of the regulars from the pizzeria. She had gotten to know some of the townsfolk quite well, just from seeing them a couple of times a week and serving them pizza and lemonade. It was surprising how talkative people could be when they began to recognize her week after week. It was one of the things that she loved about her job; it helped her feel like she really was part of the town, even though she had spent most of her life away.

Eventually they made their way into the room where the ceremony would happen. They chose seats on John's side, with Russell sitting on the aisle. Ellie had noticed that he usually chose seats where he could get up quickly if he had to, and wondered if that had to do with his responsibilities as a sheriff, or if it was just part of his personality. Russell the man was so thoroughly entwined with Russell the sheriff that it could be hard for her to tell sometimes where Kittiport's sheriff ended and where the man she loved began.

Before long, it was time for the ceremony to start. The familiar wedding march began to play, and the seated crowd rose to welcome the bride into the room. Ellie beamed at the woman. She looked gorgeous in her dress, and didn't seem able to take her eyes off of the man that waited for her at the front of the room. She glanced at John, and saw that his gaze was only for his soon-to-be wife. She didn't think that she had ever seen two people who looked more perfectly suited to each other.

After the ceremony, the guests dispersed. The people closest to the bride and groom were going up to congratulate them. Russell hesitated, then moved with her toward the doors instead. She didn't blame him; it seemed that a good third of the crowd was converging upon the newlywed couple. They would have plenty of chances to congratulate them later.

While they were waiting for the reception to officially begin, Russell pulled Ellie aside. "I don't know what your plans are after this," he said. "But if you're free, I'd like it if you would join me in a walk around the marina."

Ellie felt her heart rate increase. Was this it? Was he going to propose? She still didn't know if she wanted it to happen or not. It was too soon, but she didn't know what to say so she did what she could; she smiled and nodded, and said, "Of course."

Shannon and James found them, and shortly after that the wedding party found their way downstairs and the reception started. They found their seats, and after John's best man gave a toast, the tables were dismissed one by one to go get their food. The food looked delicious. Ellie didn't recognize the name of the catering company, and realized that if she was serious about opening a second restaurant in the future, she needed to start paying more attention to the competition in the surrounding towns. If she wanted to expand Papa Pacelli's and keep the pizzeria successful, she had to know what they were up against.

Forget business for now, she told herself. *Just enjoy the day.* There were plenty of tempting dishes to choose from: pulled pork, fish, and herb-roasted chicken. There were Swedish meatballs, hot and cold pasta dishes, and finger sandwiches similar to the ones that she had made for their boat outing. And, of course, the wedding cake.

The three-tiered cake was a masterpiece. Ellie could tell that the couple had gone all out. She smiled to herself as she loaded her plate up with other goodies. *I'll have to ask Nonna what her wedding was like,* she thought. It was just one of the many things that she had never asked her grandmother about her personal life.

She and Russell returned to their table, where Shannon and James were already waiting. The four of them had been seated at a table with two women whom Ellie didn't know. Shannon seemed to know the one that introduced herself as Jillian, and exchanged pleasantries with her. The other, a beautiful blonde woman about their age, sat morosely, picking at her food after getting back from the buffet table. Ellie watched her for a moment, wondering why she looked so dejected.

When the woman excused herself to go and get a drink, someone nudged Ellie in the ribs. She looked over to find Shannon leaning toward her. "That girl is John's ex-girlfriend. I don't think she's supposed to be here; Jill said that her boyfriend was supposed to come, but had to go in to work. That was supposed to be his seat. We're going to tell security when people get up to start dancing, but we don't want to make a scene if we can help it. Can you pass that on to Russell, so he can help in case she freaks out when they try to make her leave?"

Ellie nodded. Before leaning over to whisper to Russell, she found the woman in the crowd. Watching the way she slipped along the edges of the room, it sure looked like she was trying to avoid notice. She paused at the drink table, then hurried away when she noticed John approaching. She had every appearance of being a wedding crasher. *I hope she doesn't do anything to wreck this for them*, she thought. *This should be a joyful day for John and Leigh; she has no right to be here if they didn't want her to come.*

The woman returned with her drink, and Ellie kept an eye on her until the DJ stood up and the speakers crackled to life. Everyone's attention turned toward the dance floor where the newlywed couple was preparing to take their first dance together as husband and wife.

Leigh didn't take her eyes off her husband as he led her onto the dance floor. The lights dimmed. The DJ announced the new Mr. and Mrs. Hudson to cheers from the crowd. A slow song started to play, and Ellie smiled as she saw the happy tears on Leigh's face as she laid her head against her husband's shoulder.

They were only a minute into the dance when everything changed. John stumbled, and they both came to a halt. He leaned on his wife for a second then, seeming to slip through her grasp, fell to the floor. Everyone in the room seemed to gasp as one.

Leigh dropped to her knees next to her husband. Her face was near his, and she seemed to be whispering into his ear. He didn't move, didn't even seem to be breathing. An older lady hurried forward, announcing that she was a doctor. The entire room watched in silence. A moment later she looked up, her face pale.

"He's dead."

CHAPTER SIX

C haos erupted instantly. It seemed that Russell teleported from his seat next to Ellie to stand next to Leigh on the dance floor, he'd moved so quickly. He spread his arms out, demanding that people keep back and give the couple some space. He grabbed one person out of the crowd and ordered the man to call 911 immediately.

Ellie felt as if she was glued to her chair. This had to be some sort of terrible joke, right? John was a healthy man her age, maybe a couple of years older. He couldn't just drop dead for no reason... could he? She traded glances with Shannon, who was half out of her seat. She looked just as horrified as Ellie felt.

Despite Russell trying to keep people away, the back half of the room began to push forward in an attempt to see what was going on.

James hurried forward to help protect the couple on the floor from the crowd. Ellie realized that she should probably try to be of some help as well. She stood up, and both she and Shannon tried to convince the people around them to go back to their seats. As she was doing this, Ellie saw the blonde woman who had sat with them slip through the crowd, exiting out the back door. Her breath caught in her throat at the thought that the woman might have had something to do with this, but she was already gone by the time Ellie had moved only a few feet in her direction. There was no way to stop her before she reached the parking lot.

It didn't take long for the police to arrive. The sheriff's department was only a couple blocks away from the community center. She was relieved when she saw the familiar faces of Liam and Bethany, Russell's two deputies. The deputies pushed their way through the crowd, looking around to find the source of the commotion. It was evident that they didn't know exactly what was going on, so she waved them over and helped them find their way through the crowd to Russell. He had managed to keep the area immediately around John clear. The doctor was still standing near the man, but she didn't appear to be working on him any longer. Leigh was crying gently into his shirt. The scene was heartbreaking, and Ellie had to look away.

Gradually the chaos faded, and people began to do as they were told and settle back down. It wasn't long before paramedics came through the door, and together they loaded John onto a gurney. The doctor went with them, talking vehemently to the men as she described what she had seen. Her voice was the only one in the room. A hush had fallen over the crowd as John was being carried out.

Leigh seemed lost. She stared after her husband as if in a dream. Ellie thought that she might follow them, but instead she turned back toward the table where she and John had been sitting and sat down, staring numbly at her hands. Maybe she didn't want to ride in the back of an ambulance with her dead husband; Ellie couldn't blame her for that.

Feeling that the woman probably shouldn't be alone right now, she went over and took the seat next to her, not saying anything, but hoping her presence would be of some comfort. She looked around for Russell. She itched to tell him what she had seen, about the blonde woman sneaking out, but he was busy talking to an older couple that she thought must be John's parents; she remembered seeing them hug him after the ceremony. The woman was in tears, and her husband's jaw was clenched tightly. She knew that she could not interrupt that conversation. Everything she wanted to say could wait.

Leigh began to cry harder, and Ellie laid a hand on her shoulder. She wished that she knew the woman better, or that she could find someone who did. She searched the crowd for someone who might be able to help, and her gaze landed on John's best man, Damien. He was walking toward Russell, his face pale and confused. When he saw Leigh, he changed course and headed their way instead.

"Leigh, what happened?" he asked, kneeling on the floor in front of her. "I slipped out when you started dancing. I just saw them take John away on the gurney. What's going on?"

The woman just cried even harder. She didn't appear able to talk. John glanced at Ellie instead. Ellie shook her head, indicating that she didn't know anything more than he did.

"She just needs someone to be with her right now," she said.

"Did she say anything about what happened? I don't understand how John could..." He seemed to realize that this wasn't the time for the question, and instead dragged a chair over to sit next to the stricken bride.

Ellie made her escape, moving away from the crying woman that she hardly knew and the man who had just lost a best friend. Instead of going over to Russell and the two deputies, who were still questioning the witnesses, she saw Shannon and James were hanging back a few feet, and it was them that she joined.

"Does anyone have any answers yet?" she asked Shannon quietly.

"No," her friend said. "None of them saw anything more than we did; he was dancing, then he just fell over. I think I heard the doctor say something about a heart attack. Maybe he had heart troubles we didn't know about. Did Rayleigh say anything?"

"I don't think she's capable of talking right now," Ellie said.

"I can't even imagine.... That poor woman. I don't know how she's ever going to get over this."

"Me either," Ellie said. She glanced toward Russell. She could imagine how the woman felt; if anything happened to the man that was standing in front of her right now, she would be at a complete and utter loss.

CHAPTER SEVEN

The ill-fated wedding was the talk of the town for the next few days. Ellie felt sick every time she heard it mentioned. There had been some shocking crimes in town since she had moved back, but this—if it was a crime, and not just cruel fate—somehow felt like the worst.

She didn't have any idea how Leigh was coping, or even where the woman was. Was she still in town? Or had she gone back home? Ellie wanted to see Leigh one last time before she left, hoping to give her condolences, even though she knew that it wouldn't do much to help the pain of her loss. She figured that Leigh would probably stay for her husband's funeral, which she had heard from Russell was scheduled after his autopsy. That would be finished later in the week, hopefully.

Whenever he was working on a case, Russell usually spent most of his time at the sheriff's department. This time, he was even harder to get hold of than usual. John had been his friend, and she couldn't blame him for wanting to get to the bottom of his death. Ellie knew that he would be going over every shred of evidence: every single piece of footage from the cameras at the community center and every scrap of testimony from the witnesses, trying to find an angle for foul play. They were still waiting for the official verdict from the coroner's office, but they all knew that a healthy man did not just suddenly drop dead without explanation.

Ellie's own back and forth concerns about the possible proposal seemed suddenly ridiculous. She was glad that she hadn't mentioned anything about it to anyone other than Shannon. What was happening now was real, and it was serious. She wished that she could help Russell somehow, comfort him after the death of his friend, but she knew that the only thing that would comfort him would be finding the truth about what had happened. If John's death had been an accident—an aneurysm, a heart attack, something like that—was one thing. But if it was murder, Russell wouldn't rest until the killer was behind bars.

Shannon seemed to be thinking about John's death a lot as well. She had written an article about it in the paper, and had been much more withdrawn than usual. On Wednesday evening, after Ellie closed the pizzeria, Shannon invited her over. Ellie brought a pizza with her, as was becoming tradition. James was out surveying a site for a new contract, and Russell was still at the sheriff's department.

"Has there been any progress?" Shannon asked, taking a slice of pizza from the box. "I'm asking as me, not as a reporter. Although the paper would love to know what John's cause of death was. They keep asking me if I have any leads. The whole town seems to be waiting to see if it was murder or not."

"If he's found anything, he hasn't told me yet," Ellie said. "I know that the body's been sent for an autopsy, and they're going to do a toxicology report as well, but it's likely that we won't get any results from that for a couple of weeks. If the cause of death is found to be natural, John's body could be released by the end of the week, but if it was something more complex than a stroke or a heart attack, it could take up to a month, depending on how busy the labs are."

Her friend raised her eyebrows. "It sounds like you know a lot about all of this."

Ellie chuckled. "Not really, I'm just parroting what Russell told me. But to be honest, I haven't seen much of him lately."

"It must be hard on him, losing a friend. He knew John a lot better than I did, and I can hardly believe it myself."

"He has lost a lot of people over the years," Ellie said. They both sat in silence for a moment, considering that. Ellie wished again that she could help him, but couldn't think of a way to do so. Voicing her thoughts aloud, she said, "I just wish I could do *something.*"

"Well, we can try to talk to some people," Shannon suggested. "We helped out before that way, remember?"

"If you mean the time that we talked to those two girls who turned out to be innocent, and got into a car accident, I'm not really sure that counted as helping," Ellie teased.

"Well, okay, that's fair I guess." Her friend's lips lifted a little bit at the memory. "Well, we didn't really hurt matters any, at least, other than your poor car," she said.

"I had to get a new car," Ellie pointed out. "I can't afford to do that again. At least, not as nice a new car."

"There wouldn't be any car chases this time," her friend promised. "We'll just go and talk to people. Some people might be more open to talking to a couple of women like us than they would be talking to someone wearing a deputy's badge."

"I suppose you're right," Ellie said. "Maybe we can find someone who knows where his ex is."

She had mentioned the woman to Russell; he'd tried to find her, but no one seemed to know her name. John, whom she had dated, was dead, and no one else could tell who she was from her description alone. Ellie was certain that she was a local; she had the somewhat familiar face of someone who had stopped into the pizzeria before. She kept hoping that the mystery woman would return, but so far nothing. She had even gone so far as share a description with her employees, but no one had spotted her yet.

"Do you really think that she would've done it?" Shannon asked. "I mean, if she still loved the guy or something, killing him off wouldn't do any good, would it?"

"She might have been more crazy than actually in love with him," Ellie said. "That sort of thing happens all the time… on TV shows at least."

"Maybe she meant to kill Leigh and got John instead. It's just hard to believe he's gone," Shannon said. "I mean, he was someone that I've known for years and years. We saw him not even a week ago, on the *Eleanora*. It doesn't even feel real yet. I keep just living my life normally, then all of a sudden, I remember that this guy that I've known for most of my life just isn't around anymore. I hate it."

Ellie remained silent. She had never experienced the death of someone close to her. She hadn't known her grandfather very well, and hadn't even been in Kittiport for his funeral. He was family, but they hadn't been close. She could try to imagine how it felt, but she knew that she wouldn't really understand it—not until it happened to someone close to her.

PATTI BENNING

CHAPTER EIGHT

Shannon and Ellie hadn't had time to put their plan into motion before Ellie got a call from Leigh that changed everything. She was at work when her phone rang, and almost didn't answer the call. After hearing the other woman's concerned voice, she was glad that she did.

"Ellie, sorry, I didn't know who else to call, but I need advice. I know you and Russell are dating, but I didn't want to get the police involved with this until I knew for certain that it was something that needed more serious help," Leigh said. "Someone's been following me. I'm staying with John's parents, but they're at the funeral home picking out... well, they aren't home right now. This car has driven past the house twice this morning alone. It could be nothing, and I know I'm probably just being emotional after everything that happened. What do you think? You probably know a lot about this sort of thing since you're involved with the sheriff. What should I do?"

"What does the person look like?" Ellie asked.

"I'm not sure. They haven't gotten out of the car, and I wasn't close enough to see into the car windows. Should I confront them?"

"That might not be safe. I think you should put a call in to the sheriff's department, just in case."

"There goes the car again. You're right, I probably should just call—hold on, they're pulling into the driveway. I've got to go."

She hung up, leaving Ellie with a silent phone and a feeling of worry in her stomach. Calling out to her employees that she was leaving, she grabbed her purse and hurried to the door, making another call as she moved. When she got the sheriff department's answering machine, she let out a hiss of annoyance. The elderly secretary, Mrs. Laffere, was probably on her lunch break. She left a message, then called Russell's cell phone. This rang through to voicemail too, so she left another message. She hesitated for a moment, considering dialing 911, but decided that this probably wasn't that extreme an emergency. Like Leigh, she didn't want to blow things out of proportion.

She also didn't want to be responsible for the woman getting hurt if something did go wrong, which was why she was about to head over to the house herself. As she started her car, she placed a third call, this time to Shannon. Her friend answered, and Ellie was relieved not to have reached another machine.

"Where do John's parents live?" she asked. "I'll tell you why later. It's important."

"Unless they moved, they're in that subdivision by the park. Their house had a couple of stone lions at the end of the drive. It's been years, though, and they might have sold the place. It was a big house for just the two of them."

Ellie thanked her and hung up. It would have to do. The subdivision that she had mentioned wasn't far away from the pizzeria, and she was turning down the road only a few minutes later.

The house was easy enough to find, if it was indeed the right one. Two aged stone lions sat guard at the end of the driveway. There were two cars parked there, one of which was rusty in patches and looked out of place. Ellie parked behind it and got out. She hurried up the brick porch steps and knocked on the door. No answer came, after a few seconds she tried again. Still nothing. She hesitated a moment longer, then tried the doorknob. It was unlocked. She opened it a crack.

"Hello?" she called. She heard a murmur of voices, but couldn't make out what they were saying.

"Hello?" she called out again. "Leigh, it's Ellie. Can I come in?"

There was a pause, then she heard her name. She followed the sound to find two women seated in the living room. Leigh was on the couch, and in an armchair across from her was the blonde woman who had left the reception so suddenly.

She froze, trying to assess the situation. The woman didn't appear to have a weapon. Her mascara was runny, and her eyes were red. There was a purse on the table next to her with a crumpled tissue poking out the top.

"Sorry, Ellie, I didn't mean to worry you. You came all the way here just to check on me? That's so kind of you."

"I couldn't get in touch with Russell, and I knew I'd never forgive myself if something happened to you after all of this," Ellie said. "I'm sorry, it looks like I overreacted. I'll get going." She made to leave, planning on placing another call to Russell the second she left the house. Their missing witness had been found.

"No, no, you can stay. This is Britney. She came to apologize."

"Sorry if I frightened you," the woman said to Leigh. "I just wasn't sure how you'd react when I showed up. I kept losing my courage and driving away before I parked. I can see how that might have seemed odd."

"Why did you sneak out like that at the wedding?" Ellie asked. "Everyone has been looking for you."

"I just freaked out. I wasn't invited, and I thought I might be in trouble if I was there when the police showed up." She darted her gaze back to Leigh. "That's why I came to apologize. I shouldn't have crashed the wedding. After what happened, I realized how stupid and petty it was of me to think my being there would somehow change his mind. I should have just been happy for him. He was obviously happy with you."

Leigh took a shuddering breath. Ellie saw tears at the corner of her eyes. "We're quite the mess, the pair of us, aren't we? Here I'll show you where the bathroom is. There's tissues in there, and on the way back we can grab a strong drink from the kitchen. Would you like one, Ellie? You drove all the way over here; you're welcome to stay."

"No—" Ellie paused mid-sentence. It might be better if she stayed. For all she knew, Britney could be the killer. Leaving her alone with Leigh might put the other woman in danger, especially if Leigh had been the original target, as Shannon thought was possible. "I mean, sure, I'll stay. I won't have a drink though. I'll have to head back to work after this. Thank goodness my employees were there to cover for me."

The two women left the room, leaving Ellie alone with the empty chairs... and a purse. She bit her lip, staring at it. It was Britney's, and her fingers twitched with temptation. She needed the woman's last name, at least, and her address. Russell would still want to

73

question her. Ellie glanced in the direction the two women had gone. She heard the clink of glasses. If she was quick, she might have time.

She hurried over to the purse and pulled it open. She grabbed the woman's wallet and looked at the driver's license. Britney's last name was Elmwood. She took a quick picture of the license with her cell phone, then put it back. As she made to close the bag, something caught her eye. It was an empty plastic bag—no, not empty. There was a residue of white powder inside it. Her heart beginning to pound, Ellie snatched the bag just as she heard footsteps in the hall behind her. She stuffed the bag into her pocket, took a seat on the couch, and was pretending to be intently focused on a magazine when the two women returned.

Ellie tried to act normal for the next twenty minutes, but she kept losing track of the conversation. She couldn't keep her thoughts from the plastic bag in her pocket. The white powder could be anything, she knew. The woman could've had a powdered donut for lunch, for goodness sake. However, if she had to bet on it, she would put the odds on the powder being some sort of poison. If luck was on her side, she could just have found the murder weapon.

CHAPTER NINE

Immediately after leaving Leigh, Ellie went to the sheriff's department. Russell was still out, but she convinced Mrs. Laffere to let her wait in his office. He returned a good half an hour later. She jumped up as soon as the door opened, and fished the bag out of her pocket. He took it, looking confused.

"I heard that you called," he said. "I was just about to call you back. What is this?"

"This is evidence," Ellie said. "It's a long story, but I found John's ex and took that out of her purse."

The sheriff took a closer look at the plastic bag. He saw the white powder, and his brow furrowed. He dropped it onto the table as if it had burned him.

"You took it out of her bag?" he said.

"Yes. I didn't mean to steal anything, I was just looking for her license so I could get her full name and then I saw it. I thought it might have something to do with how John died. She seemed pretty upset about his death, and I still think it's possible that she might be the killer. She went to see Leigh. I stayed until she left to make sure she didn't try anything."

"Ellie," he said slowly, "this *could* have been evidence, but now, even if it was full of drugs that could have been used to murder John, I can't use it against her." Russell's voice raised slightly. "By taking it out of her bag, and especially by touching it with your bare hands, you destroyed its worth as evidence. Is there any proof that it's hers, other than your word? I'm guessing not. There's a reason we do things a certain way. You might have just let John's killer walk free."

Ellie was shocked. Russell had never gotten angry at her before, not like this. He had gotten upset when she did something that put herself in danger, but this was the first time she had seen his grey eyes look so hard and cold when they gazed at her. At first, she felt stung by his words, then felt a rush of anger.

"I was just trying to help," she snapped. "She could have tossed this in the trash at any point, and then you wouldn't have had it at all. You know, I tried to do the right thing and call you before going over there. It's not my fault you didn't answer." She pursed her lips, considered saying more, then decided that she might regret it if she did. Turning on her heel, she strode toward the door and showed herself out.

She was certain that Russell would call to apologize after cooling down, but her phone was still silent by the time she pulled into the pizzeria parking lot. She fretted, wondering if she should apologize, then decided that they both needed time to think about what they were going to say. It was time for her to get back to work. She would deal with Russell and whatever had just happened between them later. Right now, she had a business to run.

Russell still hadn't called by the time she left work that evening. Ellie knew that arguments were a normal thing in any relationship, but she couldn't help but feel that this was different. She had spent the past few hours coming to terms with the fact that she had screwed up. He was right, she had messed up the case. Even if the bag did test positive for the type of drugs that could be used to kill a person, Russell probably wouldn't be able to use it as evidence.

There would be no way to prove that it really had come from Britney. If that turned out to be their only evidence and a killer walked free because of it, she would never be able to forgive herself.

"I'm such an idiot," she muttered as she got into her car. "I doubt he'll ever forgive me. I wouldn't blame him. I should have just kept out of it."

She drove through town, not sure where she wanted to go. At first, she pointed the car toward the sheriff's department, then losing her courage, she drove around the block. She wasn't ready to see Russell again, not yet. Pushing the issue wouldn't help matters at all, she knew. It would be best if she just went home, but she couldn't stand the thought of pacing around her room over and over again for the next few hours until she fell sleep, worrying about all of this. She wished she could go to Shannon, but once again ran into the problem of her being his sister-in-law. It didn't feel right to share their personal issues with a member of his family.

She ended up driving aimlessly around town. The community center, now the scene of two deaths, was dark and empty. The marina, by contrast, was busy as the last few fishing boats docked for the evening. She sighed as she cruised past the sheriff's department again. Russell's truck was still there. If they hadn't just been fighting, she would have stopped by with a tall cup of his favorite coffee. She passed the building again, then cruised down a different street, passing the now empty calzone shop. Suddenly she stomped her foot down on the brake, then slammed it into reverse, parking sloppily in front of the building.

The *Sold* sign was gone. In its place was a sign that said *Hot Diggity Dawg—Coming Soon!* It looked like she had finally discovered which restaurant would be moving into the space. At least it wasn't another pizza place. A hot dog restaurant? *I'm going to have to stop in for lunch and check out the menu myself when they open,* she thought. *Hopefully the owners are pleasant. Though anyone will be better than Jeffrey and Xavier.*

Her curiosity about the new restaurant lifted some of her concern about her and Russell's fight. It was a reminder that life did go on, and she had to move on with it. Trying to imagine what Hot Diggity Dawg might look like when the renovations were done, she pulled a U-turn in the street and headed for home.

CHAPTER TEN

E llie was still buoyed by the news about the new restaurant in town when she got back to the Pacelli house that evening. She was able to set her incident with Russell aside for the moment. She pushed through the front door, greeted Bunny, stopped by Marlowe's cage to greet the big bird, then headed into the kitchen to see her grandmother.

Nonna was sitting at the kitchen table opening her mail. She looked up as her granddaughter walked in, welcomed her home, then went back to reading the letter in her hand. The kitchen smelled like blueberries, maple syrup, and bacon.

"What did you make?" Ellie asked, walking over to the stove. She saw a plate of fresh blueberry muffins sitting on top.

"Well, I was in a breakfast mood, so I made bacon and muffins, and poured maple syrup over the lot," Nonna said. "You can have the rest of the muffins. Feel free to take some to work tomorrow. You must get tired of having pizza for lunch every day."

"Sometimes it's nice to mix it up a little," Ellie admitted. She noticed her grandmother's attention was already back to the letter. "Any news?" she asked, hoping that that it wasn't anything bad.

"It's from my friend Gerry," she said. "She moved to Florida a couple of years ago with her husband, and she wants me to come and visit. It would be nice, but I don't think my old bones are up to being hauled across the country."

"Hey, I'll go in your place," Ellie joked, smiling. "Not too long ago, I was thinking how nice it would be if you had a place in Florida that we could go to visit during the winter months."

"I always thought that would be wonderful," Nonna said. "I always wanted to buy a home in Florida, even just a little place that we could rent out for half the year, but your grandfather loved this town too much to ever leave. He probably would have done it for me if I pushed the issue, but I loved him enough not to."

"You know, you still could do it," Ellie said. "Imagine, spending winter somewhere without three feet of snow on the ground."

The older woman chuckled. "Oh, don't tempt me. Like I said, I'm too old. I wouldn't make it halfway there."

"What are you talking about?" Ellie said. "With a plane ticket, you'd be there just a couple of hours."

"And then what?" Nonna asked, putting the letter down. "I would have to rent a car, and, well, I haven't driven for almost a year. I probably need to renew my driver's license, and I'm not sure if they would issue me a new one. Besides, I'd probably get lost down there. I don't know how to use those GPS systems, and I'm too old to wrestle with a map while I'm behind the wheel."

"I really would love to visit Florida, even if it's summer when we go," Ellie told her grandmother. "We could both use a vacation."

Now more than ever, she thought.

"I could visit some of the friends that have moved down there over the years. Some of them even live in the same retirement community," her grandmother said softly, as if to herself. She looked down at the letter again. "No, I really shouldn't. If I go there then I might be tempted to stay. I do love this place. It's my home."

It might be good for her to get away from the house and town that are so filled with memories of her husband, Ellie thought. It must be hard for the older woman to look ahead to the rest of her years when she was so surrounded by reminders of the past.

"I'll tell you what, Nonna," Ellie said. "I'll do some research online, and find some fares, then maybe we can talk about going. Like I said, we could both use a vacation, and I think it would be wonderful for you to be able to see your friends. Maybe I'll be inspired with some new pizza ideas while we're down there."

Ellie turned back to the stove and the muffins. She put one on a plate and set it in the microwave. While it was heating up, she grabbed the butter off the counter and scraped off a bit with a knife. She took the muffin out of the microwave, and joined her grandmother at the table. She wasn't that hungry, but she had never been able to turn down a freshly made blueberry muffin.

"So, how are things going with you and that sheriff of yours?" Nonna asked, apparently done with Florida talk for the time being.

Ellie's fingers hesitated as she tore into the muffin. The last thing she wanted to talk about just then was Russell. Would he ever forgive her for her mistake? She knew how seriously he took his work, and this case in particular was personal for him.

Still, her grandmother needed an answer. "I haven't seen much of him recently," she said honestly. "He's been so busy with the case."

"You mean that poor man who died at his own wedding?" her grandmother asked. "Was it murder?"

"They don't know yet. They're still waiting on the autopsy." She took a bite out of the warm, buttered muffin. Perfect.

"That poor man, killed just minutes after saying his vows." Her grandmother shook her head. "It seems so cruel. I'm thankful that my own wedding went smoothly. When your time comes, I'm sure it will be just perfect."

"No, no, I think I'm too old to get married," Ellie said. "I've already tried it once, and it didn't exactly work out. I'm not unhappy being single."

"There's no such thing as too old. I know someone who got married when she was just a couple of years younger than me. When the right man comes along, it will all feel perfect."

"Well then, does that mean you might start dating again?" Ellie asked, raising an eyebrow.

"It's different with me," her grandmother said firmly. "I was married for over sixty years. Your grandfather is irreplaceable to me. I don't think I could ever feel the same way about another man. Maybe— maybe—if the right person came along, I might go out to dinner with him, but it would take someone truly special, and someone who could understand my heart would always belong to someone else first."

It sounded as if her grandmother had already given the matter some thought. Ellie smiled. She hoped that the older women would find someone she could date, even if they only had dinner together every once in a while. She knew that the years of her grandparents' marriage hadn't been perfect, but there was no doubt that they had truly loved each other. One day, she wanted that for herself. Despite her own protestations that she was okay with being single, she knew that she didn't want to spend her life alone.

CHAPTER ELEVEN

Ellie took her time getting ready for work the next morning. She kept glancing at her phone, hoping that Russell would call or text, but nothing came through. She was beginning to worry in earnest now. Should she make the first move? She decided to give him more time. If he hadn't said anything by the next morning, she would call him.

To make up for running out the morning before, she had told Jacob that she could open on her own. It was usually quiet for the first hour or two anyway, so she didn't mind. Once she got the ovens turned on, the sign out front lit up, and the door to the patio unlocked, she got to work on making one of their new pizzas of the week, both to make sure that she had the right amounts of everything, and to give her something to snack on between customers. She had eaten another of the blueberry muffins that morning, and didn't think she wanted one for lunch as well.

The pulled pork pizza had been Jacob's idea: tender pulled pork slathered with sweet barbecue sauce, and covered with melted Gouda and mozzarella cheese. The Gouda had a hint of smoky flavor to it, which tied the dish together perfectly. She made herself a good old Chicago-style deep-dish pizza, and pulled a piece off to munch while she waited for the first customers of the day.

She was surprised when one of the first people that came in was someone that she recognized. Damien, John's best man. She last seen him at the wedding, attempting to comfort Leigh.

"I was hoping to see you here," he said, approaching the counter.

"Me? Why?"

"I figured if anyone would have answers about what happened to John, it would be the sheriff, or you."

"I really don't know anything more than anyone else. If there is anything new with the case, Russell would be the one to know. Have you been to see him yet?"

"I thought I'd try you first; I was going to grab lunch anyway. Besides, I don't know if he would talk to me. Don't police usually have to keep quiet about open cases?"

"There are some things he probably wouldn't be able to mention, but I'm sure he'd be able to tell you something. At least what he'll be telling the papers. I really don't know any more than you do at this point." She hesitated. "You knew him better than I did. Did his family have a history of any medical issues?" It was the sort of thing that Russell would normally have shared with her, but since she hadn't had a chance to really talk to him since the wedding, she would just have to find out herself. She found herself hoping that the answer was yes. If the death was determined to be from natural causes, then the case could close.

"Well, John's grandfather passed away from a heart attack, and his mother had to have heart surgery a couple of years ago, but if something was wrong with him, he didn't tell me," Damien said.

Maybe he really did just have a heart attack, Ellie thought. *The excitement of the wedding could have caused it. It's sad, but it would mean that no one was at fault.*

"I just want closure, you know?" he added. "He was my best friend. I want to know that he didn't suffer. If someone killed him… well, I would hope that the police would have some leads by now."

"Do you know why anyone would want to hurt him?" Ellie asked.

"I've got no idea," the man said. "He was a good guy. No enemies that I knew of. My gut tells me it was a natural death, but I just want to hear it from the officials before moving on."

"Do you know someone named Britney Elmwood?" Ellie asked. She knew that she probably should just let the man go on his way, but she couldn't help herself. Shannon had a good point when she said that a casual conversation might be more likely to get people to open up than direct questioning by an authority. Talking to the police was bound to make people anxious; talking to the lady at the pizza place was an entirely different story.

"I recognize the name," he said. "Oh, yeah. John used to date her. Blonde lady, right?"

"Yes, her. How was she, back when they dated?"

"You think she might have something to do with this?" Damien asked, raising an eyebrow.

"I don't know, but I do know that she was at the reception, and sneaked out right after he collapsed," she said, lowering her voice even though they were alone in the restaurant. "It just seemed suspicious to me. You said that he didn't have any enemies—were you counting exes in that?"

"Man, Brit was crazy," he said. "Totally off her rocker. Ask anyone, I'm sure they'll tell you the same. That's why he broke up with her. They hadn't dated for years. I had almost forgotten about her. She would send him a message every now and then, but we both thought she had moved on. I guess not, if she crashed his reception."

"A crazy ex who still had feelings for him," Ellie said. "That definitely sounds like someone who might have had a reason to want to hurt him. Or Leigh."

"It wouldn't surprise me if she decided that if she couldn't have him, then no one could." He paused, then looked at her sharply. "Wait, you don't mean that you think she might go after Leigh next?"

"It was just something my friend mentioned," Ellie said. "That maybe Leigh was the target all along, and she got the wrong person."

He frowned. "I should get going. Thanks for the conversation." He gave her a quick nod, then turned and walked away, leaving without even glancing at the menu.

Ellie retreated to the kitchen, keeping her ears open for the sound of the bell on the door. She had a lot to think about. It was sounding more and more like Britney might be the suspect if John's death had indeed been foul play. Someone so obsessed with someone after years of being apart might be just a little crazy. Maybe even crazy enough to do what Damien said, and kill him so he wouldn't end up with someone else.

She thought about the woman's red eyes and the tissue in her purse. Unless she was faking it, Britney was taking John's death hard. She knew that someone unbalanced might take out her pain on the very person she thought she loved, but in this woman's case, it might be more likely that Shannon was right and Leigh had been the target. She was glad that she'd ended up staying with her until Britney left. *There is still the chance that she could go back and try to finish the job,* she thought. Her skin prickled. This was something that she couldn't keep to herself. Russell had to know. She couldn't stomach the idea of putting someone else's life in danger just because she was too embarrassed to talk to her boyfriend again. Taking a deep breath, Ellie grabbed her purse off the counter and pulled out her phone. She turned on the screen, to find that Russell had already called her and had left a voicemail.

CHAPTER TWELVE

E llie pulled into Russell's driveway and sat in her car for a moment, feeling nervous. She had no idea how this evening was going to go. His voicemail hadn't told her much, nor had the short conversation she had had with him when she called him back. He had simply asked her to come over that evening after work. With some idea of what to expect, she would have been able to brace herself. As it was, things could go either way. She would just have to wait and see.

With a sigh, she grabbed her purse and let herself out of the car. She saw his adopted cat, Sookie, sitting in the window. The cat had actually adopted him. She had appeared one night during a storm, and hadn't left his side since. Ellie liked the cat. At least Russell had some company, someone to talk to, even if that someone had four legs and fur.

The sheriff opened the door before she had a chance to knock. He welcomed her inside. She slipped off her shoes, hung her purse on the hook by the door, then turned to him. However, he had already disappeared. She followed the noises into the kitchen, where she found him unpacking a couple of bags of take out.

"Sorry," he said over his shoulder to her. "I had hoped to come back in time to make dinner, but the time got away from me. I picked up some soup from that café by the sheriff's department. They were just about to close. I'll have to remember to leave an extra big tip next time I stop in."

"You didn't have to," Ellie said. "I would've been happy to bring something from the pizzeria if you wanted food."

"I wanted to apologize to you," Russell said. "I figured this would be a good way to do that. I'm sorry, Ellie, I really am. I shouldn't have snapped at you."

Ellie didn't bother trying to hide her relief. She smiled at him and said, "I'm sorry too. I shouldn't have gone into her purse. If I had thought before taking it, I would have realized that touching what might be evidence could make things more difficult for you. I hope I didn't wreck the investigation."

"Well, it turned out that there won't be an investigation. The coroner's report came in; the cause of death was a heart attack. Given the family history, he's labeling it a natural death."

"That's good," Ellie said, though she wasn't sure if that was the right word for it. "I just mean, I'm glad that it wasn't murder. Does this mean his family will be able to have the funeral?"

"Yes. They've already scheduled it for Saturday. I was actually hoping you would come with me."

"Of course," Ellie said. She tried not to think about how very wrong it was that not even a week after his wedding, John was going to be buried. The man hadn't deserved to die so soon. He had deserved many happy years with his new wife.

"I would have apologized even if the coroner had found something that pointed to foul play," Russell said after a moment. "I don't want you to think I'm only apologizing because I was wrong about it being murder."

"Russell, you don't have to explain anything. I'm just glad that my mistake didn't wreck everything. Let's enjoy our meal together, and be glad that all of this is behind us."

They ate outside on the back patio until the mosquitoes chased them in. The cat followed them, hurrying through the screen door as if she was worried she might get shut out for the night. *I wonder what was in that bag,* Ellie thought as she finished the last of her soup. Russell might have already sent it off to be tested, but she wasn't going to ask him, not then. She didn't want to bring it up again. Whatever the woman was into, it hadn't cost anyone his life. That was all she really cared about.

After dinner, they went on a walk around the neighborhood. Russell lived on the outskirts of town, on the opposite side of Kittiport from the Pacelli house. It was a quiet area, but the street was well lit by streetlamps. By then, it had gotten chilly enough that the mosquitoes had mostly given up for the night. He lent her a light jacket to wear. She was reminded for the first time in days of the ring box—or what she had thought was a ring box. Would she ever find out what that had been?

Her thoughts drifted back to the wedding, and she realized that she had forgotten to tell Russell about her encounter at the pizzeria earlier that day.

"By the way," she began, "Damien, John's best man, stopped in the pizzeria today. He wanted to know what progress you made on the case. He'll be glad to know it wasn't murder. He seemed to think that Britney, John's ex, might have been involved."

"What did he say about her?" Russell asked, taking her hand to guide her around a pothole. He didn't let go.

She related the conversation to him. She didn't know why he was so interested; the case was all but closed now from the sound of it.

He paused and turned toward her she finished talking. "Do you remember Britney's full name? Yes, I know what the coroner said," he added as she opened her mouth, "but it's not impossible that he was given some sort of poison that might have caused the heart attack. If something did happen, we need to figure it out before he's buried."

"I wasn't going to argue," she said. "I was just going to tell you that I took a picture of her ID. It's on my phone, and I'll send it to you when we get back."

He chuckled. "Sorry. I shouldn't have doubted you. I know I'm probably barking up the wrong tree, but I just know I won't be able to let this case go unless I'm thorough. Something still feels off, but for the life of me, I can't pinpoint what exactly it is."

CHAPTER THIRTEEN

When Russell stopped in at the pizzeria the next day, he didn't have any good news to share with her. Even knowing Britney's address, he couldn't find her. She wasn't at her house, and had taken a few sick days off of work. She could be anywhere, and without a warrant, there wasn't much Russell could do to find her.

"What about the bag?" she asked, meaning the plastic bag with the white residue on it.

"I sent it out for testing. It probably won't get resolved until next week at the earliest. We had to send it into the city, we just don't have the equipment locally for that sort of testing." He sighed. "For all I know, it's baby powder. If we bury him, then find evidence later that he was killed... well, I don't want to be the one to issue the order to exhume his body."

Ellie winced at the thought. It was bad enough that Russell would have to see his friend get buried. It would be worse if he had to watch his body be exhumed.

Saturday arrived, but no updated news came with it. The funeral would go ahead, and Ellie could only hope that John was able to rest in peace after being lowered into the ground. A week ago exactly, the man had been sitting on the *Eleanora* with them. The six of them had eaten together, shared jokes and stories, and none of them had imagined the horror that waited for them the next day. Now, one of them was about to be put into the ground. It was horribly sad, but it was also frightening. The thought of how easily life could end, without any warning at all, made Ellie want to focus on the present even more. No one's future was guaranteed. She shouldn't put off spending time with her loved ones, because one day soon it would be too late.

That trip with Nonna is happening, she told herself. *I don't know if I'll get another chance. She's done so much for me; taking her to Florida is the least I can do in return.*

She wore a somber black pantsuit to the service. Nonna came with her, but joined a group of her own friends when they entered the funeral home. Ellie found Russell and waited with him out front until Shannon and James arrived. They went back inside as a group.

The viewing was held before the service. John looked no different than she remembered. The mortician who had prepared his body had done it well, and there were no signs of the autopsy. He really did look like he was sleeping. She bit her lip, trying not to think about how very alive he had been seven short days ago, and moved along. Russell paused by his friend for longer than she had, but eventually he, too, turned away.

"The service starts in an hour, then after that the procession to the cemetery leaves. His parents invited us to the burial, but if you would rather not go, I would understand."

"We can do whatever you want," she said. "I don't mind going to the burial with you." The truth was, she would rather not go, but she wasn't about to abandon Russell to go on his own. Death wasn't the sort of thing that she could avoid just because she was uncomfortable with it.

It wasn't long until one of Russell and John's mutual friends pulled him into conversation. He tried his best to include Ellie in it, but she didn't know any of the people they were talking about. Deciding to go and find Shannon, she mumbled something about visiting the bathroom. She did indeed visit the facility, taking a few minutes to check her phone and freshen up before rejoining the viewing. It took her a few minutes to find her friend. When she did, the other woman was deep in conversation with someone that Ellie didn't know. Unwilling to interrupt, Ellie walked past, looking out the windows instead. It was sunny out, with just a few white, wispy clouds in the sky. It seemed incongruous somehow; on such a sad day, it should be grey and rainy. It didn't feel right to lay someone to rest in the sunshine.

A pair of figures toward the front of the room caught her eye. They were standing side by side, the man with his arm around the woman's shoulders. Both were looking down at the casket where the man was laid out. She recognized the woman's auburn hair; it was Leigh. She wasn't certain, but she thought that the man standing beside her was Damien.

She felt a stirring of sudden suspicion. Damien, John's best man. Damien, Leigh's ex. Damien, who would have had access to all of

John's drinks and his plate of food. Damien, who, if he still had feelings for Leigh, might have had a very good reason to want his best friend dead.

A motive doesn't make him a killer, she thought. *He hasn't raised any red flags in the police investigation. I'm sure Russell would have looked at him as a suspect.* Yes, he had his arm around Leigh, but that was because this was an impossible day for her. She needed his support to get through it. They were still friends, that much was evident. What she was seeing now was simply one friend comforting another.

Something about his visit to the pizzeria a couple of days ago nagged at her. She hadn't been suspicious of him at the time. Now, seeing them together, it made her wonder. Had he been so interested in the case because he was waiting to hear whether or not he was going to get away with murder? And at the wedding, just after John had died, he had asked Ellie if Leigh had said anything. Had he been checking to see if she had seen him slip her husband something?

Ellie shook her head, trying to convince herself that she was connecting dots that weren't supposed to be connected. She forced herself to turn away. Russell. She needed to find Russell. She would mention it to him, but that was it. She wasn't here to do any investigating, and she wasn't about to bring unnecessary drama to the funeral of a good man.

She turned, surveying the room for the sheriff, and instead saw another familiar face—one that she hadn't been expecting, with a veil over her hair, face tilted downward. It was Britney. She was standing by the door and her eyes were fixed on front of the room, where Leigh was standing. She was fumbling through her handbag for something. Ellie's heart skipped a beat. She was caught between two potential murderers, but only one looked like she might be reaching for a weapon. If she didn't act fast, she could find herself witness to a second murder.

CHAPTER FOURTEEN

W here was Russell? Ellie looked around for him, but he was nowhere to be found. Britney suddenly shut her handbag and started moving forward. Ellie was frozen. If Britney had a gun in her bag, or even a knife, she could pose a serious threat to anyone here. She was making a beeline toward the casket, but when Ellie looked back, she realized that Leigh and Damien were both gone. Had Britney been forced to wait to pull her weapon out because they walked away, or had she been innocently looking for a lipstick or bottle of lotion in her purse?

Darn it, Russell, where are you? Ellie thought. This was his job, he should be here dealing with this, not her. The last thing she wanted was to cause a scene at his friend's funeral. Of course, someone getting shot or stabbed would cause a scene too.

With a sigh, Ellie gave up on her visual search for the sheriff and turned to follow Britney. The least she could do was to keep the woman in sight. If she approached Leigh, then Ellie could try to stop her. If she was just here for the viewing, well, watching her wouldn't hurt anything.

Britney stared into the casket for a long time. Ellie could see how sad she was. Once again, she found herself wondering if this woman could have killed the man that she had so clearly loved. But if it wasn't her, then who? His best friend? Either way, John had been betrayed by someone who had claimed to care about him. *If he was even murdered,* she found herself thinking. *Russell and I might both be wrong. The coroner said it was a heart attack. He was a man in his mid-forties with a family history of heart issues. It's not impossible that his death was as simple as that.*

She sighed and scanned the crowd again, looking for Russell. She really just wanted to share her concerns with him. He would know what to do. He always did.

When she turned back to check on Britney, the woman was gone. *Shoot. She can't have gone far,* Ellie thought. She had already lost track of her boyfriend, but somehow losing sight of a potential killer was even more embarrassing. How on earth had the woman managed to slip away so quickly?

She approached the casket and saw what she had missed before; a door just around the corner from the viewing area. That would explain how Leigh and Damien and Britney had vanished from view in just a few seconds. She shot one last, desperate look out across the room for Russell, then decided that this was too important to wait until she found him. Hoping that she wasn't about to make a fool of herself by walking into a supply closet, she opened the door and slipped through, shutting out the sounds of the funeral home behind her.

She found herself in a small bereavement room. It was empty, and there was nowhere for anyone to hide unless they could fold themselves up enough to fit under the couch. There was another door across the room, however, and this one had a red exit sign above it. Ellie sighed and, hoping that it didn't lock behind her, pushed her way through.

She found a beautiful garden behind the funeral home. It wasn't in full bloom just yet, but the air still smelled sweet with the scent of flowers. Surprised at this unexpected little slice of paradise, she followed the stone path. It was a beautiful area for the bereaved to go to recover from their tears. She would love to have a garden like this herself, but knew that she would never keep up with all of the work it would take to maintain it.

The find was so unexpected that she almost forgot what had caused her to stumble upon it in the first place. When she heard the honking sound of someone blowing their nose, it reminded her that she wasn't alone. There was at least one other person in this garden, and she very well might be a murderer.

Ellie slowed her pace and walked as silently as she could in her heels. The path wound its way around a large, slightly overgrown bush, and she paused to peer through the branches. She saw blonde hair, and knew that she had the right person. The only question was, now what? It was easy to forget that, despite all of her suspicions, Britney might be completely innocent in all of this. She had followed the woman out here in the off chance that Britney intended to hurt Leigh, but neither Leigh nor Damien were anywhere to be found. She didn't even know if they had come out here. Britney might really be the grieving woman that she seemed to be.

It was, she knew, time to tell Russell what she was doing. This was a personal case for him, and he would want to be involved, whether or not she was right about Britney.

Retreating down the path far enough that, with luck, her voice wouldn't carry, she pulled her phone out of his pocket and dialed his number. She wasn't surprised when it went to voicemail. Russell was in the habit of keeping his phone on vibrate, one of the few things he did that she wished he wouldn't. *The whole point of having a cell phone is so people can contact you when you're out,* she thought as she waited for the greeting message to end. *What's the point of even having the thing if he never notices it going off?*

When the beep sounded, she left her message, telling him where she was and why before hanging up and returning to the spot behind the bush. She didn't know how long Britney would stay out there, but with luck the woman would retreat inside before the service started.

It startled her when her phone rang loudly in her hand. She pressed the volume rocker down to mute it out of reflex, but it was too late; through the branches, she could see Britney straighten up. *If Russell keeps his phone on vibrate too much, then I don't silence mine often enough,* she thought, annoyed at herself.

117

"Is someone there?" Britney called out. Ellie shoved her phone in her pocket and walked around the bush. It wasn't difficult to look embarrassed.

"Sorry, that was me," she said. "I stepped out to make a call. I forgot my ringer was on. Good thing I hadn't gone back inside yet."

"It's okay, I was just startled." The other woman wiped at her eyes with the back of her hand. "I came out here to cry, I didn't expect to see anyone else."

Ellie opened her mouth to tell her that she was going to head back inside, when she heard another voice coming from somewhere else in the garden.

"There's no one else here, Leigh. That ringtone was probably from someone in the parking lot. Just tell me whatever it was that you brought me out here for. The service is going to start soon, and we can't miss it."

She was almost certain that it was Damien's voice, and there was no doubt that the woman who answered him was Leigh.

"Damien, I know how John died, and it wasn't an accident."

CHAPTER FIFTEEN

Both Ellie and Britney froze. It seemed like they waited an eternity before Damien responded.

"What are you talking about, Leigh?"

"He didn't die of natural causes." Her voice cracked. "I just… I thought you should know."

The pizzeria owner slid her eyes over to the blonde woman still sitting on the bench. Had she killed him? If Leigh gave her name up, would Britney try to escape? Ellie knew that one place that she did *not* want to be was right next to a killer that was about to be exposed. She began inching back, putting space between herself and the woman who was listening so intently.

"It was a heart attack. That's what they told everyone. Why do you think it was something else?"

"It *was* a heart attack." Her voice twisted, as if she had started to cry. "But it wasn't from natural causes. I caused it. I did it. I killed him."

"Oh, Leigh, don't say that. Just because his heart attack happened after your wedding doesn't mean it happened *because* of your wedding. For all we know, it could have happened while he was on the couch watching football. At least when he passed, he was surrounded by the people he cared about."

"You don't understand what I'm saying," the woman said unevenly. Her voice shook, and Ellie thought that it wouldn't be long before she began to sob. "I killed him, Damien. I did it. I poisoned him during the toast."

The garden fell silent. *No,* Ellie thought. *It's not possible. She's just confused. She doesn't know what she's saying.* Damien seemed to have the same thought.

"Of course you didn't. Whatever silly wedding tradition you broke, that's not why he died. Come here, let's go back inside. You shouldn't miss his service."

"Stop it!" Leigh snapped. Ellie heard the crackling of small branches breaking. Had she shoved him. "Why aren't you listening to me? I killed him. I put poison in his drink. I did it so I could be with you."

Britney stood up in an instant and began moving down the path toward them. Ellie hissed at her to come back, but the other woman ignored her. She followed, realizing the irony in the fact that she was now trying to protect the woman that only a few minutes ago she had thought capable of murder.

She wasn't quick enough to catch up to Britney before Britney reached Leigh and Damien. The blonde woman didn't hesitate for even an instant. She strode right up to Leigh and, before the woman could react, punched her in the face.

Leigh stumbled backward. She reached out to Damien to balance herself, but he jerked his arm away from her. She ended up half falling into a prickly bush, but didn't seem to notice the brambles that got caught in her dress. She wiped her hand across her mouth and looked in shock at the back of it, which had come away bloody.

"I'm going to kill you! How could you do that to him?" Britney shrieked. She pulled back her hand to punch the woman again, but Ellie grabbed her by the arm—not to protect Leigh, but because the widow had just slipped a bottle of pepper spray out of her purse. It wasn't lethal, but she wasn't eager for any of them to be sprayed with it.

"I was being kind to him," Leigh said, trying to disentangle herself from the bush with one hand while keeping the pepper spray pointed in front of her like a shield with the other.

"You're a crazy freak!"

"Shut up, you don't know a thing about love," the auburn-haired woman snarled. She gave up on her dress and simply yanked herself free, ripping it in the process. "Do you really think he would be happier if I had broken up with him? On the eve of his wedding? The man died happy, and as painlessly as any of us can hope for."

"He's not happy now. He's dead!" Britney tried to yank herself out of Ellie's grasp. The pizzeria owner let go of her arm, but managed to get both arms around the other woman's waist before she lunged forward again. One of Britney's elbows hit her in the ribcage and she grunted with pain. It was tempting to just let her go, but she knew it wouldn't be the right thing to do. There was no telling who would end up getting hurt.

"Well he's not sad either, is he?" Leigh was breathing heavily. Her lip was still bleeding from the punch, and that, combined with her torn dress, made her look like an asylum escapee. Her eyes darted from side to side, looking for a clear path away from them. It was obvious that this confession hadn't gone how she had planned. She hadn't expected witnesses.

"You... tell me you aren't serious." Damien was staring at her, his face a mask of shock. "I don't... why would you..."

"I thought it was the answer to our problems," she said, her eyes flicking back up to his. "After you kissed me that night, I knew I couldn't go through with the wedding. How could I, when I was in love with you?"

"You could have broken up with him like a normal person, you psycho," Britney snarled.

"I didn't want to hurt him! Why can't any of you see that? I cared about him. I loved him. I just wasn't *in* love with him."

"You didn't want to hurt him, so you killed him." Damien's voice was flat. "That's your version of love, is it?"

"Just stop it!" Her voice climber higher. "All of you, stop. None of you know the truth. His heart… he had heart disease. It used to be under control with medicine, but it had been getting worse. The surgery that the doctors suggested didn't have a high chance of success, and he didn't want to die on an operating table. He didn't want anyone to know, he thought they would treat him differently. If I had called off the marriage, *that* might have killed him. But he wouldn't have died happy then, would he?"

She was crying again. Ellie thought that the tears were real; Leigh really might have thought that she was making the kinder choice.

"How did you do it?" Damien asked. His voice was thick, and his hands were shaking. Ellie tried to imagine what he was feeling.

From the sound of it, he had shared a kiss—and maybe more—with his best friend's fiancée a few nights before his wedding. Then he had watched that same friend's body carried out on a stretcher, only to discover that the woman for whom they both had feelings had been the murderer.

"Potassium chloride," Leigh said. She took a shaky breath and let it out slowly. "It was an oral solution. I poured what would have been a fatal dose for a healthy man into his wine. He didn't finish the drink, but with his heart condition, it was enough to cause a fatal arrhythmia. You have to believe me, Damien, he felt very little pain. It was a good way for him to go; I made sure of it."

The man nodded, his gaze far away. "There's just one thing I don't understand," he said slowly. He raised his eyes to hers. "Why would you tell me this? How the hell could you think that I would feel anything—*anything*—other than disgust after learning that you murdered my best friend?"

Leigh inhaled sharply as if his words had physically hurt. "I couldn't keep lying to you. You deserved the truth. I'll never lie to you, never."

"You'll never get the chance to," he said. He stepped toward her. Ellie expected Leigh to raise the pepper spray, but instead her fingers opened and it dropped to the ground. She looked at the man in front of her, and took a hesitant step back, as if she wasn't sure what she was reading in his eyes.

Ellie and Britney watched, mesmerized, as Damien reached up to wrap his hands around Leigh's throat. She didn't move until he began to squeeze, then she began to struggle. The movement broke the spell, and Ellie realized what she was witnessing.

She spotted the pepper spray on the ground and did the only thing that she could think of—she grabbed it. After fumbling for a moment, she got the nozzle pointed the right way and depressed the plunger. A fine orange mist sprayed out, covering both Damien and Leigh's faces.

Damien let Leigh go immediately, and both collapsed on the ground in fits of violent coughing. Ellie took in a breath to shout for help, but something painful caught in her throat and she choked on her words as her lungs tried to expel the blowback of the spray. She stumbled away until she felt someone's hands on her. She let the person guide her back through the gardens. Within minutes she was leaning against the sink in the ladies' room splashing water into her face. Britney was standing behind her, wringing her hands.

"Get Russell," Ellie managed to croak. "Sheriff."

Britney slipped out of the room, and Ellie hoped that she knew who she was looking for. She tried to take a deep breath, but ended up coughing again. When she finally looked back up, she saw that her eyes were red and puffy. She had barely caught the finest mist from the spray. She couldn't even imagine what the two people who had caught it directly were feeling just then.

She didn't have to wait long before Russell came through the bathroom door, Britney on his heels. He came over to her immediately and looked into her face.

"Did you wash your eyes out?" he asked.

"Yes. I think I'm okay. But the others, they got it worse," she said. "Leigh killed John. She confessed everything. Hurry, before she gets away."

He hesitated for a split second before nodding. "Stay here with her," he demanded of Britney before he left the room. Ellie squinted at herself in the mirror. The killer was found. The case was closed. John would be able to rest in peace after all.

EPILOGUE

"I love you both so much. I'm going to miss you. Don't forget me, okay?"

Ellie hugged Bunny and planted a kiss on top of the dog's head before turning to Marlowe. The parrot had her face pressed against the bars of the cage and was staring out at her with one sharp gold eye.

"I'm sorry. We would bring you with us if we could."

The dog had already trotted off to sniff each and every corner in the pet sitter's house. The bird, on the other hand, seemed to sense that something was up. It broke Ellie's heart to see her clinging to the cage bars like a prisoner. Marlowe was being silent, but she could see the fear of the unfamiliar place in her eyes.

"We'll be back in no time at all," she continued, wishing that the animals could understand her. If she could just *explain* to them that they were only going to be gone for a week, it might make it better.

"They'll be fine," the pet sitter said. She was a young woman with bright red hair and an easy smile. Bunny had taken to her immediately at their first meeting, and even Marlowe seemed to accept her.

"Thank you so much for watching them, Sierra," Ellie said. "You'll send updates every day?"

"Yep. I'll let you know how they're doing every morning. I've got the vets' numbers on the fridge, and the address for the emergency vet is already programmed into my phone. You've seen my yard— it's completely fenced in. Even Bunny won't be able to find a way to squeeze through. I'll only be pet sitting one other animal during the time that you're gone, and it's a cat. We'll be fine. Your job is to relax and enjoy yourself."

"I know you'll take care of them, it's just hard to leave." She opened her mouth to call Bunny to her for one last cuddle, then thought better of it. The papillon had discovered a basket of dog toys and was happily digging through it. It was probably better if she didn't draw too much attention to the fact that she was leaving. "I guess that's everything. You have the emergency number, right?"

"The sheriff's number?" Sierra grinned. "I sure do. These will be the most well-protected pets in town. They'll have their own mini-vacation while you're away."

Ellie smiled, then turned away when she felt her lower lip quiver. The animals would be fine. She was going to come back for them in a week's time. Why did she feel so guilty, like she was abandoning them?

"I'm leaving now, for real this time," she promised. "Goodbye, and thanks again. I'll be back next Saturday. Have fun, you two!"

Before she could hesitate any longer, she stepped out onto the porch and pulled the front door shut behind her. Her car was parked in the driveway, and Nonna was sitting in the passenger seat. The elderly woman smiled brightly as Ellie slid into the driver's seat. An excited twinkle was in her eye.

"Are we ready?" she asked.

"That was the last stop before the airport," Ellie said. "Florida, here we come."

Made in the USA
Middletown, DE
23 August 2023

37238228R00076